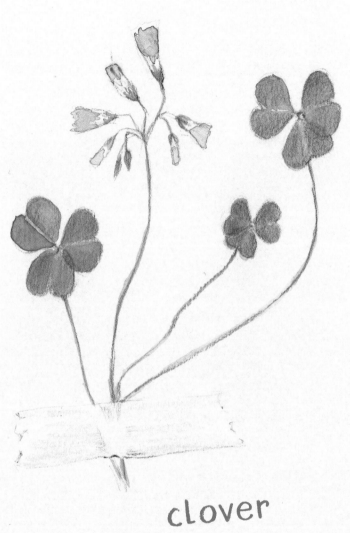

clover

CUENTO DE LUZ

For Álvaro, Pablo, and Xabi, for many more walks with you . . . through the countryside and through the city.
—Paula Merlán

For those who know how to reveal the value of details to others.
—Concha Pasamar

This book is printed on **Stone Paper** that is **Silver Cradle to Cradle Certified®**.

Cradle to Cradle™ is one of the most demanding ecological certification systems, awarded to products that have been conceived and designed in an ecologically intelligent way.

Cuento de Luz™ became a **Certified B Corporation** in 2015. The prestigious certification is awarded to companies that use the power of business to solve social and environmental problems and meet higher standards of social and environmental performance, transparency, and accountability.

Something's Happening in the City
Text © 2021 by Paula Merlán
Illustrations © 2021 by Concha Pasamar
© 2021 Cuento de Luz SL
Calle Claveles, 10 | Pozuelo de Alarcón | 28223 | Madrid | Spain
www.cuentodeluz.com
Original title in Spanish: *Algo está pasando en la ciudad*
English translation by Jon Brokenbrow
ISBN: 978-84-18302-50-3
1st printing
Printed in PRC by Shanghai Cheng Printing Company, July 2021, print number 1838-14
All rights reserved.

Something's Happening in the City

By Paula Merlán   Illustrated by Concha Pasamar

Hannah decided to go for a walk
through the city streets. A gentle
breeze was blowing.

Her dog, Pippin, was by her side.

The city was beautiful in the springtime. April was Hannah's favorite month.

Insects buzzed busily through the air, and the sun was shining brightly.

As she walked along, Hannah began to realize that something strange was going on in the city.

She saw Carol, her neighbor, walking toward her with her head bent down.

"Good morning!" Hannah said happily.

"Oh, hi," Carol said without looking up. She didn't pay any attention to Hannah as she walked past.

Hannah looked at all the wonderful sights around her.

"The clouds are so fluffy this morning!" she thought. "And the birds are having a singing contest on the roof!"

She kept walking, until she saw something unusual. A group of children were sitting on a park bench, but they weren't talking or looking at each other.

"Something strange is going on in the city, Pippin," said Hannah, "and I'm going to find out what it is!"

Pippin wagged his tail. He wanted to know what was going on, too.

Hannah continued on, then saw a man who was also looking down at the ground.

"I wonder what he's so interested in, Pippin," she said.

Just then, she noticed a flash of red up in a tree.

A squirrel! She imagined how far it must have traveled and all the adventures it had before reaching the top of the tall tree.

Hannah turned the corner and saw an old bookshop.

She looked through some of the books that were in a box outside. They were full of stories of faraway places, with deep, dark jungles or snowy mountains.

In a stroller near the store was a beautiful baby with a gentle smile that seemed to fill the world with color.

A woman walked past, and Hannah realized she hadn't even seen the baby. The woman seemed to be far too busy looking down at something else.

Hannah thought, "Maybe she's under some kind of magic spell!"

With all these thoughts running through her head, Hannah soon reached the park.

"Everything's so beautiful! Look at all the trees, and the flowers by the pond!" she said.

"Woof!" said Pippin. He always agreed with his best friend, Hannah.

Two boys ran over, laughing as they played together. Their father was looking down and seemed to be very busy with something. What was going on?

Hannah was about to find out.

She crouched down behind a tree and watched as the man walked past.

So that's what it was!

The man was holding something in his hand.

It was as if some powerful force was preventing him from looking up.

Hannah set off for home. As she walked,
an idea began to take shape in her head.

"I wonder if it'll work. Let's give it a go!"
she said to Pippin.

The next day, Hannah set off on another walk with Pippin around the city. She was looking for someone.

There she was! It was Carol. Hannah had something in her hand: a photograph. Carol looked at it, and a smile spread across her face.

"Those are the most amazing clouds I've ever seen! Thank you, Hannah!" replied her neighbor happily.

"Clouds are magic," said Hannah. "If you just use your imagination, you can turn them into anything you like!"

Carol and Hannah sat down on a bench and looked up at the sky. "That cloud over there looks like a musical note!" said Hannah. "And the one next to it looks like a heart!"

The wind blew in the trees. Carol's phone was deep in her bag, but it didn't matter. Hannah and Carol talked about the clouds, the birds, and all sorts of things. Life was wonderful!

Hannah had a folder full of photos for anyone who wanted to look at them. There were photos of flowers, clouds, rivers, bugs, and trees.

The city is beautiful in the springtime. All you need to do is raise your eyes to see it.

dandelions